December, 2001

Dear Reader,

I found this album of photographs hidden in the floorboard of my home. It's an old house, full of secret little nooks and crannies, but until this discovery I had never come upon anything quite so mysterious or lovely. As I opened the album, it was with great amazement that I realized the house in the photographs is indeed the very house I live in now!

These photographs were taken on Christmas Eve 1901. They are of the Gordon family, who lived in the house a hundred years ago. While the captions under some of the pictures seem to have been written by the youngest Gordon child, the pictures themselves were taken by his uncle. I have been unable to track down any relatives of the family who might be able to shed more light on this album, or why it's been kept hidden for all these years. The best explanation, I think, is that the family was wary of the publicity that most surely would have surrounded them. Or maybe they had made a promise of secrecy to St. Nicholas himself? That seems possible, for, as all the world knows, he is notoriously camera-shy. Or it may simply be that the Gordons wanted to preserve the spirit of the holiday—that Christmas is about believing with the heart what we cannot see with our eyes.

I had these photographs authenticated by several experts, who tell me that they are indeed real. (I knew that already, of course!) May this album find a place in your hearts!

Happy Christmas!

— Raquel Jaramillo

My Family

The Night Before Christmas

Words by

CLEMENT CLARKE MOORE

Pictures by

RAQUEL JARAMILLO

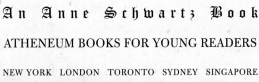

An Anne Schwartz Book

ATHENEUM BOOKS FOR YOUNG READERS

NEW YORK LONDON TORONTO SYDNEY SINGAPORE

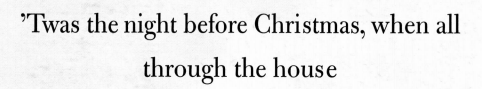

'Twas the night before Christmas, when all
through the house
Not a creature was stirring, not even a mouse;
The stockings were hung by the chimney with care,
In hopes that St. Nicholas soon would be there;

The children were nestled all snug in their beds,

While visions of sugar-plums danced in their heads;

And Mamma in her 'kerchief, and I in my cap,

Had just settled our brains for a long winter's nap;

When out on the lawn there arose such a clatter,

I sprang from the bed to see what was the matter.

Away to the window I flew like a flash,

Tore open the shutters and threw up the sash.

The moon on the breast of the new-fallen snow,
Gave the lustre of mid-day to objects below,
When, what to my wondering eyes should appear,
But a miniature sleigh, and eight tiny rein-deer,

With a little old driver, so lively and quick,

That I knew in a moment it must be St. Nick.

More rapid than eagles his coursers they came,

And he whistled, and shouted, and called them by name;

"Now, Dasher! now, Dancer! now, Prancer and Vixen!

On, Comet! on, Cupid! on, Donder and Blitzen!

To the top of the porch! to the top of the wall!

Now dash away! dash away! dash away all!"

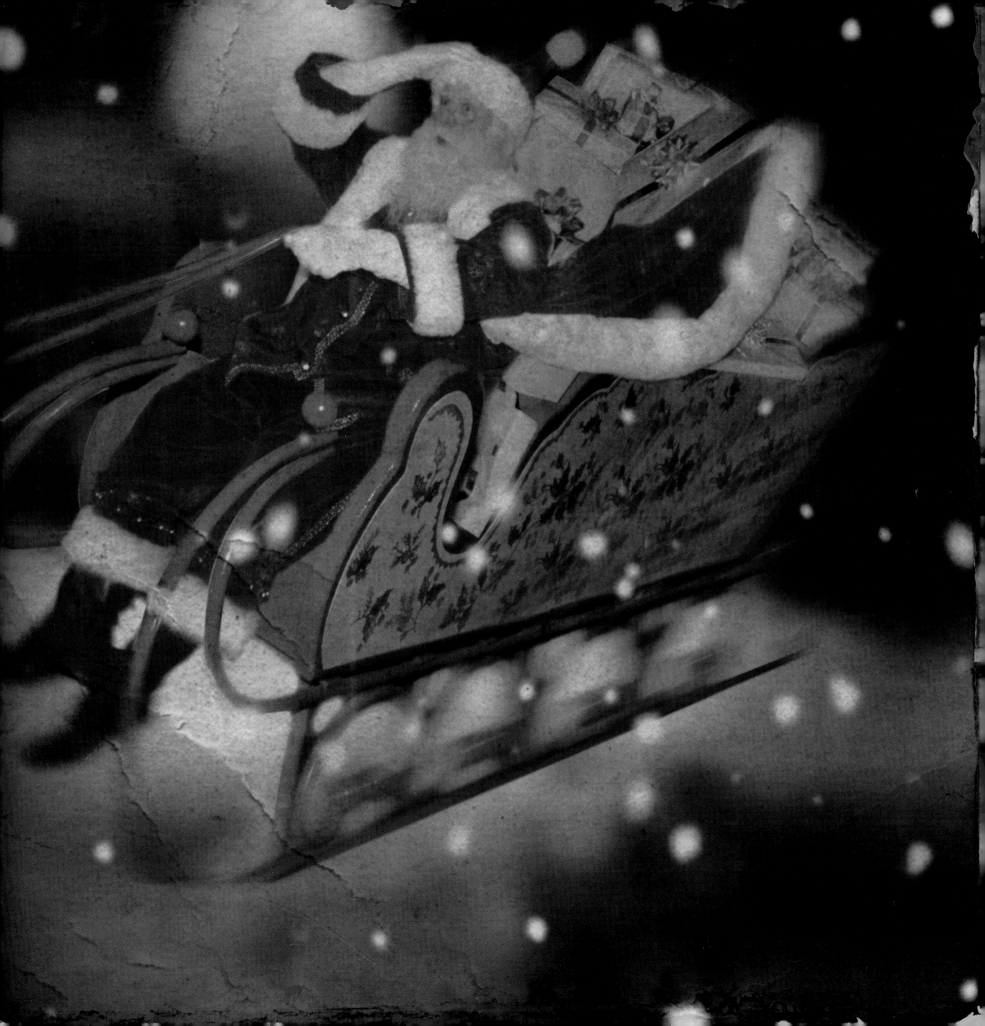

As dry leaves that before the wild hurricane fly,

If they meet with an obstacle, mount to the sky;

So up to the house-top the coursers they flew;

With the sleigh full of toys, and St. Nicholas too.

And then, in a twinkling, I heard on the roof

The prancing and pawing of each little hoof—

As I drew in my head, and was turning around,

Down the chimney St. Nicholas came with a bound.

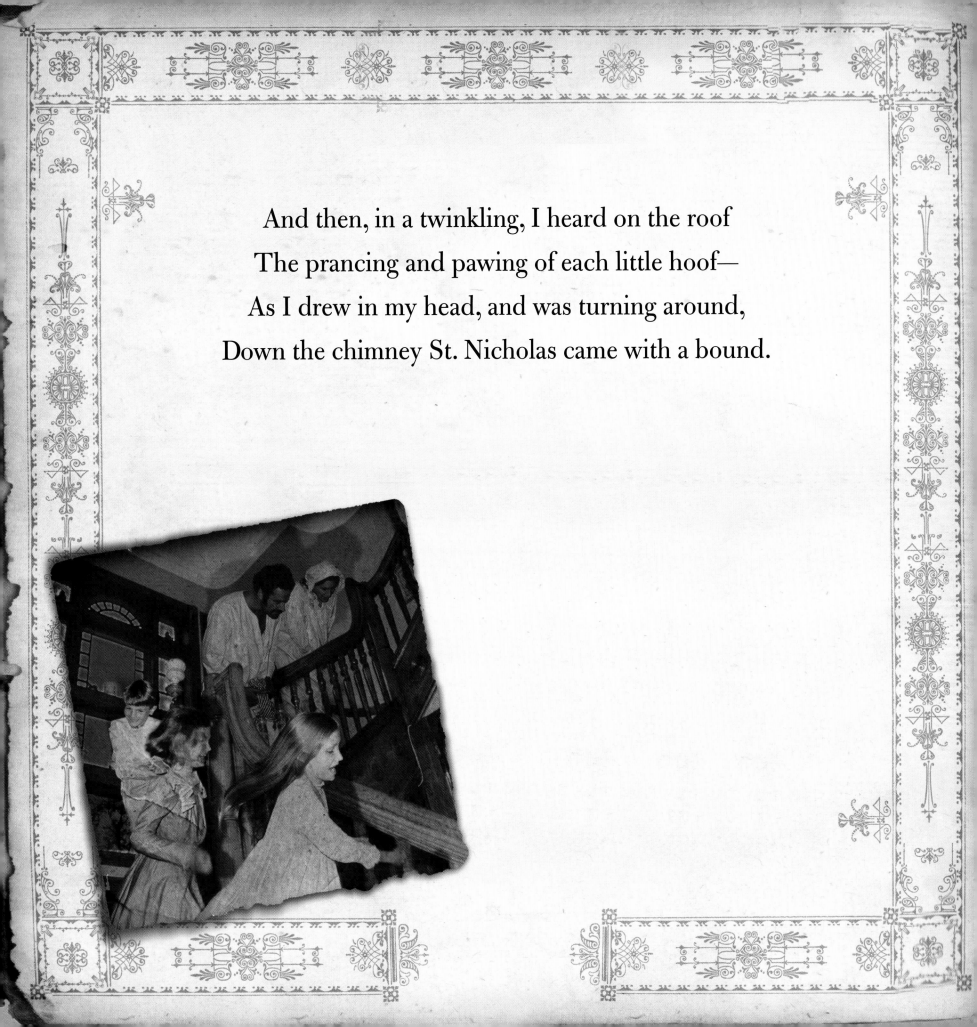

He was dressed all in fur, from his head to his foot,

And his clothes were all tarnished with ashes and soot;

A bundle of toys he had flung on his back,

And he looked like a peddler just opening his pack.

His eyes—how they twinkled! his dimples how merry!

His cheeks were like roses, his nose like a cherry!

His droll little mouth was drawn up like a bow,

And the beard of his chin was as white as the snow;

The stump of a pipe he held tight in his teeth,

And the smoke it encircled his head like a wreath;

He had a broad face and a little round belly

That shook, when he laughed, like a bowl full of jelly.

He was chubby and plump, a right jolly old elf,

And I laughed when I saw him, in spite of myself;

A wink of his eye and a twist of his head,

Soon gave me to know I had nothing to dread;

He spoke not a word, but went straight to his work,

And fill'd all the stockings; then turned with a jerk,

And laying his finger aside of his nose,

And giving a nod, up the chimney he rose;

Christmas morning!

He sprang to his sleigh, to his team gave a whistle,

And away they all flew like the down of a thistle.

But I heard him exclaim, ere he drove out of sight,

Happy Christmas to all, and
to all a good night.

THIS BOOK IS DEDICATED TO MY HUSBAND, RUSSELL,
WHO MAKES ALL THINGS POSSIBLE.

ACKNOWLEDGMENTS

I would like to thank Lee Wade for being an angel of clarity. Many thanks to Anne Schwartz for her vision and
guidance on this project. I needed it. My thanks to Brady White, for being such a wonderful Santa;
to Liz, Mark, Jack, Celine, and Janine, the perfect Victorian family; to Joyce Baldassari and Robert Pritchard
for being so generous with their beautiful home; to Pablo Vengoechea, for his expertise on landmarks;
to Helen Ussner, for her gorgeous costumes; and to the Kaplans of The Prop Company.
My gratitude to Kenn Russell, for all his creative input and energy (and for keeping me honest).
Words can never express my love and sincerest thank-you to my mother and father, Nelly and Marco Jaramillo.
Every Christmas was magic. *Mami, gracias a mi abuelito.*
My last and biggest thank-you is to my son, Caleb, who set so many marvels into motion by being born.

A BRIEF NOTE ON THE TEXT

This poem was first published anonymously under the title *A Visit from St. Nicholas* in 1823 by New York's *Troy Sentinel*. It was an immediate hit,
and was reprinted by popular demand in numerous publications and books. Not long after its initial publication, the poem started to be accredited
to Clement Clarke Moore, a Bible professor in New York, who was said to have written it as a Christmas present for his children. Although Moore
later published the poem in an anthology of his own poetry, the authorship is still disputed even to this day. Since the poem has been printed and
reprinted hundreds of times with minor variations in punctuation and spelling, most specifically regarding the spelling of the reindeer's names, this
edition is following the version Moore himself transcribed in longhand in 1856, with minor exceptions.

Atheneum Books for Young Readers
An imprint of Simon & Schuster Children's Publishing Division
1230 Avenue of the Americas
New York, New York 10020

Illustrations copyright © 2001 by Raquel Jaramillo
All rights reserved including the right of reproduction in whole or in part in any form.
Book design by ONE THOUSAND JARS
The text of this book is set in Bulmer, Goodfellow, and Old English Text.

The illustrations were rendered using a combination of traditional and computer-enhanced photography.

PRINTED IN THE UNITED STATES OF AMERICA
2 4 6 8 10 9 7 5 3 1

Library of Congress Card Number: 2001086467

ISBN 0-689-84053-5
Based on the poem "A Visit from St. Nicholas" by Clement Clark Moore

Christmas morning!

Close view of reindeer
(I think this was Blitzen)

My favorite picture
of St. Nick

First glimpse of Santa